In the Mist Of Fire

Nathalie Gribinski

RUSTY WHEELS MEDIA
THEY KEEP TURNING

First Printing, 2018

Rusty Wheels Media, LLC.
P.O. Box 1692
Rome, GA 30162

ISBN: 978-1-7328400-0-3 (Paperback)

Printed in the United States of America

-Disclaimer- Any resemblance to actual persons, living or dead, events, or locales is entirely coincidental. While some instances or thoughts may appear real, they are merely a perception of reality, brought to life by the author and artist.

For my marvelous mother who has been present all along
with her supporting love.

For my wonderful niece, Julia, who always inspires me
and sparked the idea for the Candles on Vacation.

For projects past, and this precious book.

Let there be many more in our future...

-Marc, RWM

Table of Contents

With a Pen

With a pen, one feels strong
Everything is permitted
With words, touching paradise
And above all, never reaching death

With a pen, it's much easier
Everything becomes unreal
With rhymes, we fly over an archipelago
With commas, we suddenly change islands

With a pen, everything is so different
With a plume, we fly to a dream
We often forget that it is brief
This life that we change into a diamond

With a pen, it's never the same
We invent laws, we recreate poetries
With a point, we change our mood
We create many renewals

With a pen, we think of the sun
It shines strongly between the lines
We walk between the vineyards
We rediscover other wonders

With a pen, we dry our tears
We can join infinity
Without paying anything
We create roads, we create weapons

With a pen, we draw love
We can scratch the bad days
We feel powerful forever
We forget that we live in an oven

With a pen, I loved life
I painted another color
Assigned another heart
I have abolished the limits of immensity

The Melting of Harlequin

It is a cold day in winter. And yet, Harlequin is melting.
She has a tear in her eye. A blue tear. A tear of hope, maybe.
She is lonely. What could have happened to her devil ear? Are her thoughts
so sad that her whole body is transforming?
Her nose is expanding.
Her foot is bloody from walking through her dreams to find a friend.
No one to talk to.
But she won't look back. She might be fearless after all.

There is a long journey ahead. How old could she be? Will she live eternally?
Maybe the tear is going to expand into an oasis that she will never feel.
She will walk for decades searching for love and never find it. Getting close without
ever touching it. Maybe, it will be an ocean to jump into, and she will find peace,
immersed in water, surrounded by beauty, by magic, by diamonds, by colors.
Maybe she will be learning fish-talk and meet some friends at last
and find herself at peace.

So, tear of hope or tear of despair? You decide.

Toad Slingshot

On a cloudy day of summer, at dusk, a storm destroyed
the village of Tarassad. People were flying in the sky, animals
were swimming in the river of fire. When the storm was over,
there was no one left except a Toad and the Prince of Blackness.

"My name is Barbida," said the Toad.
He was distraught, frightened, with a touching expression
on his face.
"The winds brought us together. What's your name?"

"I am Sycroline, the Prince of Darkness. We are very lucky
to be the only survivors. I see you have a slingshot in your hand.
Goodness came to you as you were going through the turbulence.
If you can throw the stone right in my hand, I will find a princess
in the village of Plutarch, and you will, at last, meet a frog.
She will give you children and love.
I can see your despair. Don't be afraid. Fear is paralyzing."

"And if I miss," said Barbida?

"Impossible. Did you see the size of my hand?
But hurry, when sunrise comes, my hand will shrink.
If you miss, I will have to eat you. And I don't really like frogs!"

The Strange Animal Fair

"Have you seen my fox"? asked a little girl to a gentleman who walked
in the Swallow Park.
"He does not look like a fox," added the girl.

"So how do you want me to help you?" shouted the astonished man.

"It's easy. He looks like a fox-monkey."
"I saw a monkey," answered the amused man. "But he looked like a chameleon."
"Chameleons do not look like anything since they transform according to their moods.
So, you are a liar and I suspect you stole my fox."

"Mr. Constable, this man stole my fox."
"What does he look like, pretty young lady?"
"I do not know anymore," answered the little girl.

"Go see the strange animal fair. You'll find elephant-eared dogs, rabbit birds,
bulls with one eye, seal-footed flies, illuminated hippocamps like Christmas balls,
rat-fish, three-fingered goats, electric bears, goose-headed cows, weeping lizards,
wolves with velvet hearts, camels on bicycles, horses on wheels,
shark-winged leopards, jumping mice, three-beaked ducks,
laughing owls, kangaroos with hats, and many
other creatures that will enchant you."

"You can accompany me?" asked the little girl.
"No," answered the Constable. "I lost my wife at the pig fair."

Swan of Hell

A swan fell from the sky. Ageless, he could be one hundred or one thousand years old.
In his destructive universe, he was mean and vicious.

Every time a beautiful bird sat atop a cloud,
the swan would chase the bird into his dark castle.

In the swan's castle, there were thousands of caged birds, singing melancholy songs
and waiting for rescue. No one ever came.
The swan reigned like a king: Powerful. Confident. Eternal.

One day, just before sunrise, he dreamed of stealing many more birds from their
paradise, their home. In his dreamy haze, the swan sang a dark, haunting melody.
The melody reached one caged bird- a tiny, beautiful swallow with a broken
wing- who heard and knew immediately of the swan's dream.

The swallow alerted all the other poor victims. They needed strength and faith to build
the nest of evasion. They had to hurry and escape before the swan awoke.
One bird had an idea.

"Let's convince him that it is even better on earth. That there are more birds,
more than he could ever imagine. Let's change his dream!"

Easier to say than to do. One bird remembered, when he was in the clouds, that
his parents told him that anything is possible when courage, faith,
and infinity would embrace themselves.

So, the birds sang.

They sang of infinity, the endless adventure of life, and the beauty of eternal bliss.

They sang of courage, the collective bravery found in harmony with one's friends.

They sang of faith, the knowledge that their song would never lead them astray.

As they sang, birds from other cages joined them, bringing thoughts of freedom,
roaming, and endless skies. Their song delicately caressed the dreaming swan's ears,
setting upon him images of paradise.
And the swan ripped from his evil dream, fell from the sky.

The cages opened, and the birds flew free, all the while, singing their song.

Dream of a Wasp with Slippers

If only I could be a servant!
I am dreaming in my slippers. A giant hand tries to touch me.
I am sure it is a King. I will be the royal servant.
But where is the Queen? This castle looks like a maze.
I will get lost for sure.

And that's great, that's all I ever wanted. Get lost and be closer
to discovery and adventure. And if I never see the Queen, it will be ok.
Maybe there is no Queen. I just want to be loyal to the hand who rescued me.
The King has more than one heart. He probably has more than one Queen.
That's why I can't see her. She is all over the place.
She IS the King.

I swim in the lake close to the forest, waiting for my first mission to complete.
Suddenly, a baby King appears. He is very skinny, with organic shapes,
and a red head. Comforted in a white bubble, he looks like a wise baby.
Can a baby be wise?

I will probably have to serve the baby King as well...
I get off the lake, put my slippers back on, and walk to introduce myself.

His name is Amirad. "Hello, I am the majestic servant. How can I help you Amirad?"
"The King stole my heart," said Amirad, whispering.

"I can give you mine," I replied. "I don't need a heart to be a servant.
I don't need compassion or sympathy or love. I just want to be a servant.
I am a follower."
I pulled out my heart and offered it to Amirad.

Then I woke up.
I was sad to have left the dream. I couldn't be a servant anymore.
Why did the King steal Amirad's heart? I will need to get back to my dreams.
I will need to get my heart back and understand why Amirad got his heart stolen.
Is it possible to come back to a former dream?

13

Candles on Vacation

Every person and every creature has a birthday. All are born on a certain day
and will die on a certain day. Days in between are full of life. In Africa,
these days are far too few for some who simply can not take the heat.
Candlesticks melt away and their remains are left,
untouched, on a cake.

Mr. and Mrs. Candlington watched from heaven, their four kids melting away as
they reminisced their short but memorable childhoods. They observed their kids
go through the same miniaturization they went through themselves.

The beginning of the parents' process was abrupt. They attempted an escape
from their wooden table in the basking sun to leave for a colder climate called Alaska.
They heard a rumor that, in Alaska, barbarian ogres with fur as white as the
frosting which covers them for hours, tumble in the wild.
They walk an even whiter ground made of billions
of tiny crystals, each no bigger than the head of a pin.

Mr. and Mrs. Candlington longed for this place and took a leap of faith
off their wooden table. Their life was then cut in half.

One day, when the Candlington children were meeting their end, an elderly rabbit
walked by and suddenly stopped. He looked up and fell to the ground.
His heart slowed, his pupils grew, and his soul departed from his body.

"Look, said Mrs. Candlington from the heavens, "a soul nearby is
floating up to join us in the afterlife. That poor rabbit."

Mr. Candlington frowned, then a wave of ideas crashed upon him. "Come here!"

"Sweetstick! Mrs. Candlington said as she rushed to her husband. "Are you okay?"

Mr. Candlington grabbed his Mrs. and jumped onto the back of
the spirit which was rising up to greet them. Life was returned to both the rabbit
and Mr. and Mrs. Candlington. The couple rode down from the sky
on their stead, and they rushed
to save their children from the perilous lands of buttercream.

As they approached their wooden table once again, their kids could not believe
their eyes. Their parents were alive and heading towards them.
"Look up in the sky!" said the youngest.

The Alien's Eye

Do you see us? I see you.
I know, I am not the normal creature. I am multidimensional.
I come from the abstract galaxy. Stars are dancing in my soul.
As they say... I have a mind of my own. And a body made up of funny shapes
who talk to each other. Some are drawn by reason, some are shaped by passion.
When they struggle with each other I am inhabited by an ant.

Do you see her dressed all in green, with yin and yang eyes?
Or maybe this is a lizard. Does it matter, after all? I just know I am not alone,
and I feel haunted.
Also, do you see the black clock reflecting on my silhouette? Can you hear it?
It tells me when it is time to close my eye.

Then, for a couple of hours, my dreams are immersed in salvation
and there is an angel over my thoughts, bringing peace over my soul, bringing
joy in the depth of my beautiful mind. Could the angel live with me, live in me?

When my eye opens, I am in despair. Could the angel steal the clock?
Stop time forever? She is pretty and slim. All draped in orange.
But she is not a magician, neither is she a fairy or a wizard.
She is a comforter of the darkness. Her bright color shines and envelops
my spirit in a perfect harmony.

But what is happening? The clock is ticking again, my eye opens,
and suddenly I realize that the beast is whispering in my ear
that she had a talk with the angel and she will leave my body forever.
I don't want the angel to come back. I want my eye opened
forever because I love life, finally alone, pure!

Whirlwind of a Feast Day

In a graceful dance, a flicker of hope and joy, four majestic mermaids portray a colorful swirl. It has been raining for decades, and today, finally, the sun shines on a dreamy landscape, just for you.

They are agile and charming. Their fluid gestures draw in the wind joyous shadows that give an impression of calm and tranquility.
The movements twinkle as if the sun had settled in a soothing eternity.
Heat waves cover a warm and voluptuous atmosphere, all around you.

A bed of coral upholsters the marine ground. There, a blue snake, a black hippocamp, an orange duck, and a rainbow tapir watch the spectacle with great emotion.
You share in that pensive glance and shimmer.

A long long time ago, they were all mermaids themselves. They whispered in your ear, a kind of buzz and hum that vibrated your inner self, the story of their greatest chance of shimmering hope, and biggest downfall.

As they were dancing on a sunny day, there was no elegance or refinement in their composition. Their movements were jerky. There was no rhythm whatsoever, no liveliness. They were trying very hard. Their dancing would not impress anyone.

So, they have been punished by the God of Aesthetics to never dance again.

They are not jealous, or bitter, they are not envious, they are just mesmerized by the scenery, and hope it will last forever.

Mask of Joy

On a clear day of spring, as you were walking into the forest,
a chick named Duffy landed on your shoulder.
You knew his name because it was printed on his subtle wing.
His parents must have feared he could get lost. But there was no number to call.
He seemed disoriented. He was hurt and thirsty.
You brought him to your house and lay him on a cradle. But Duffy was not used
to being caged up in a house, and so he died. You were so sad that you cried for days.
Your face looked like a wet pumpkin.

In your closet was a mask your uncle brought from Africa. You were told it
would bring happiness but could be used only once, and for only one year.
Was it time to use your joker?
From the window, a bird, that must have been a canary from
looking at his yellow coat, flew and landed on the mask, singing.
It was a sign. Canaries are happy birds. You put the mask on and
suddenly were filled with joy. You could almost not bear it.
The dead chick came back to life. The canary was melodious.

But the mask started to talk.
"If you want your joy to last all your life, you have to kill the chick!"
You were filled with jubilation.
You always wanted to kill but were afraid of the repercussions.
You delicately covered the bird with a napkin and strangled him.

Now, you will always be joyous, no matter who you kill or love.
And the canary was crying in front of this petrifying spectacle.
Canaries are not always happy, and neither are you.

Vacuum Cleaner with Elephant Head

The jungle is full of surprises. I went on vacation in the depths of the Amazon
and I walked in the garden of discovery for days. Trees welcomed me,
and branches bowed before me.
I was walking like a Prince in another universe as I forgot all the problems
related to human life. It was intense, but I had peace in my mind.
I felt light, free, without any destination to stop my waking dream.
In the foliage, the creepers enveloped the wind in a silver silence.

For the first time in my life, I knew everything was right. I had found the truth.
I was never going to leave the jungle. Who would push me away?
There was only nature and beauty.

Suddenly, I heard a noise. An elephant sounded.
As I became silent and amazed, he approached.
When the elephant was one meter away from me, it stopped dead.
We were face to face.
Nobody spoke. Even the trees appeared silent.

The shadowy creepers moved like madmen towards the elephant.
They wrapped him from feet to neck to the point that his body
became a creeping plant. A loud noise exploded in the sky.
I was hypnotized.
As in a robotic dance, the creepers began to become statues.
No more life.

What remained looked like a vacuum with an elephant's head.
But how could that be?
A vacuum cleaner in the jungle? The elephant's head moved.
I approached and gave it a peanut. What have I done?
It was a nasty hoover. The elephant vacuum went crazy.

He started following me in the forest and I ran fast, trying to escape the monster.
He wanted to swallow me or transform me into a statue.

The jungle is full of surprises. I think I will go to the beach next year
and eat ice cream under the sun.

The Schizophrenic Indian

I heard that I have a condition. I heard that I am different,
that maybe I can't fit into this world. I haven't always been like that.
There was a time when communication was easy, rewarding even,
and I was satisfied with my thoughts and actions.
People around me were engaging.

One day, as I was preparing for a party, my parents screamed
at me for not dressing properly.
It was a shock. But they never screamed at me.
Nobody was really looking at me.

I thought my parents were in town. I got scared.
I changed my clothes, put on my blue outfit, the one I feel
the most comfortable wearing,
and went hiking in the valley of thoughts.

It was the first day of winter. As I was going through the valley,
I heard a noise coming from my body.
I was walking on a fish. The fish was stuck to my foot.
My foot was the fish, but fish live in water.
What was he doing in the valley of thoughts?

Then, an orange light appeared in front of my eyes.
There was smoke coming out. But I couldn't smell anything.
Circles of bright light were dancing, celebrating life.
I have never seen such beauty.
But there was nothing.

I had a vision. I got scared again. I went down the valley,
ran as fast as I could to get home and changed my clothes.
I lay down on my bed.

I heard my parents shouting at me:
Dinner is ready!
There was fish on the table.

Goose Playing with Guitar

But is she really a goose? She has an elephant foot with green nails.
Could she be a peacock?

Four angels, all dressed in shades of blue, are singing with her.
The red angel is deaf.
A little bit apart from the group, he watches the spectacle.
He can see. He can feel.

In spite of his impairment, he experiences the warmth
and observes the dance of passion.
His red coat protects him from a violent, shifting wind, blowing like
a trumpet in the sparkled sky. He is fragile. He cannot lose the other angels.
They are the light of his soul. They protect him.
He wouldn't survive all alone.
He might even die.

Now the goose is playing a sad song.
The blue angels won't sing anymore, they don't even want to listen.
And yet, the spectacle bursts with color.
The red angel, not affected by the music that he cannot perceive,
continues to dance, enchanted by the magic of the scene.
Really? A goose playing guitar?

The blue angels are depressed. They no longer chant, they no longer dance.
The red angel feels suddenly the strongest of them all.
He is ready to fly through the wind to find other souls to protect,
other geese to play, maybe piano or saxophone.
He is sad for the blue angels, hoping that the goose will play
some happy songs once again.

The red angel is free. His weakness drove him to deliverance.
His difference got the best.

The Decline of the Magic Shoe

"What a catastrophe! There are so many obstacles to avoid, and I need
a good shoe to cross the river of hopes. The rocks would hurt my feet."
The little-painted bunting is trying to reach his family on the other side
of the blue forest, and he notices the multicolor magic shoe.
The little bird courageously starts a conversation.
"I need your help." He is the smallest, but he is strong and determined.

"You stay here shoe, magnificent, arrogant. You decide who to dress up
and who to let go barefoot like a little birdy in the crazy jungle.
You have magical power. You know it, you take advantage of it.
Your shoelaces dance in the swing of the wind,
like threads of desire. Each of them stimulates your leather-brain
and give you the energy to save the world from blisters.
Yet, you do nothing!

Do you realize how selfish you are? Do you know the pain of walking in the deep
forest on the branches of mystery, without ever knowing where the trail goes
because the voyage never ends?

You can change things.
You can give birth to more magic shoes for all inhabitants of the forest.
All mermaids of the rivers would even find peace
and comfort to go on with their journey.
You probably have seen it all. You have magic powers,
but you can not dream anymore!"

The magic shoe got surprised and responded to the bird.
"No one has ever dare talk to me that way!
I am the one who decides where to spread the magic.
I have the privilege of choice.
And now you come to make me feel guilty?

Do you even notice how old I am? My power is diminishing.
I have used it for decades. I can not even save myself, so be quiet here, or go to sing
in other horizons."
Who is selfish now? The one who hopes or the one who can not give?

The painted bunting got ashamed of himself and was sad. No more magic.
Never again.
He apologized and left quietly on its way to his parents, hoping that his wings
would bring him to the destination and that his feet would hold the trip.

Caribou with Skis

In northern Canada lives a Caribou that has detached from his herd.
He longs for a little isolation and wants to have new experiences.
He loses himself in the forest and runs into people who are skiing.

What a funny thing, he said to himself.
I would like to have fun like them and go down on winding, snowy slopes,
but I do not know where to get my skis.

He quickly had a genius idea.
Why not use my antlers as skis and tie them to my hooves?

He rushed into a tree to break his rack and hit a crying branch.
The Caribou tied his antlers to his hooves and the branch arched before him.

"What is the cause of your grief?" asked the Caribou to the branch.
"I will never be able to ski," the branch replied. "I have arthritis
and my doctor has banned me from exercise."

"But a branch does not ski," answered the Caribou. "You are too fragile.
You want the impossible. Go build nests for unfortunate birds that have
no refuge and stop boring me with your problems."

Despite tears running down the branch like miserable torrents,
the Caribou disappeared into the windward forest to join
a group of skiers who were frolicking in the snow.
He encircled them, showing himself proud and strong.

A child asked him.
"Mr. Caribou, I lost my parents, could you help me find them?"
"I went astray from my herd to be free," responded the Caribou.
"I can not take care of you."

He left the child alone in the middle of the mountain and went away lighthearted
to find his loneliness, far from people.

A crying branch, a lost child, but who do they think I am?
I want to have fun at the heart of my precious freedom.
People think only of themselves.
They see a Caribou skiing and are not surprised at anything!
But in what world are we living?

Mask of Hatred

It's party time in the village. The inhabitants play in a mist of joy
to celebrate the shortest day of the year. The stars blend in a dark blue sky.
They form circles of light that dance around the wind, a galaxy of blue shadows.
A blue rabbit, magicians, fairies, and princesses illuminate
this rush of happiness like a diamond.

In this peaceful atmosphere, a man hidden behind a silk wall contemplates
the show with sadness. He does not have the right to participate. He is dressed
in a purple ornament that sparkles like an Orchid.
He was punished by the mask of hatred that was jealous of his beauty and freedom.
The mask, triumphant, has locked him forever in the cellar of oblivion.

Will the mask of hate wake up to throw its venom on another happy spirit?
It's a melancholy song of a lost cicada that catches his attention.
He wakes up and jubilates with cruelty in front of this enchanting spectacle.
He sees the blue rabbit whose tail swirls in the wind.

The mask of hate has scrupulously chosen its wicked demon for this deed.
The one who will kill the rabbit is dressed in orange peels. The hunt begins under
the kneaded eyes of the inhabitants. The mask covers all their heads.
They jostle and panic as he plunges them into devil dreams.

The blue rabbit is the only survivor of this tragic episode. He tries to escape
the newly-formed wizards. He is almost to the ramparts of the city when a violent
wind brings him back to the smells of death and the colors of iron. He finds himself
next to the hatred mask and bravely begins a conversation
in the hope to kill his murderous instincts.
He tells him the story of the prince of forgotten lands with details as striking
as mines of fire. He doesn't stop talking.

The mask of hatred falls asleep.

Cheerfulness comes back to the city. The faces are revived and the bodies
of merry puppets dance to the sound of bells.

The mask of hatred will not wake until dawn, when the stars will have
already spun. The night will wake up the day which will dazzle the village
of delicate sparks with scarlet color.

But dawn never came back. The deep night will remain forever, and with time, the mask
of hatred will fade and give way to joy and the brilliance of hearts in search of beauty.

Shark on Wheel

A shark family swims in the deep sea. They are waiting for fresh prey to feed the
whole family. A sudden noise draws them, and to their surprise, a car has fallen
into the sea. The shark father rushes to see if people are stuck inside.
A mermaid manages to disengage and escapes out the door.

The shark is furious. How to catch her? The car starts talking to him.
"Oh, my poor shark! The siren is already far away. If you want to catch up with her,
why not take my wheels and tie them to your body? They slide on the waves like
soap bubbles."

The shark hurries to tie the wheels on his body and starts chasing the siren.
By rolling with all his heart and cutting through the waves, he manages to find her.
He stops in front of her. She remains calm.

"I will kill you, beautiful mermaid, and bring you back to feed my family."
"What is your name?" the siren asks.
"My name is Karocus, the Killer of the Sea. I will not ask your name since soon,
you will be no more."

"Wait before taking my life," answers the siren. "I find you very different from
other sharks encountered in these deep waters.
Why are these wheels attached to your body?
It is very charming, and you are so elegant."
She dresses him with more of her finest compliments.

The shark, flattered, is no longer hungry. Nobody, even his wife, has ever spoken
to him that way. The mermaid dances before him, turning her head beautifully.
Karocus feels that he is falling in love.

"Do you want to follow me to find my family?" Karocus asks.

"No," says the siren. "Your wife would be jealous and kill me.
Take me on your back and ride as fast as you can.
You have to give up your killer instinct to survive in my
world where there is only beauty and loyalty. The faster you ride,
the more you will become nice and the more you will be loved."
The shark disappears like an arrow as the siren strokes his back.

They end up beaching on an island. But when Karocus removes his casters,
his killer instincts make him jump on the siren.
He devours her, at once, without thinking of his family.

The Eyes of the Casino

"It's your turn," shouts the fire fairy who turns the wheel of torture with impressive energy.
"Match and don't lose!" she screams.

People gather around the game. Passionate, hypnotized, they dream of the time
when their color will win. They have only one chance.
On this devil wheel, lights glitter, chips are illuminated, and Crystal beads dazzle
the paradise of desire and uniqueness.
It is a world where hopes and dreams swirl, like silver veils enveloping
the most delicate duchesses.

Two big eyes are watching the machine. Big tears flow when there are no winners.
In this casino, no one earns money. They win an identity, a dream, a miracle.
And it is a miracle to win.

The fire fairy starts spinning the wheel again. This time, there is a winner.
A little man with a round head who had played the color yellow.
Big eyes have tears of joy. The little man has earned the right to fly over sunflower
fields every day at dusk. He leaves the game, light as the wind, within his pockets
a piece of gold that he will have to throw in a river for his dream to come true.

Another winner who had played green yelled with joy when the wheel stopped on
its color. He had the right to turn into a crescent moon when he would fall in love.
And one more champion who had earned the chance
to sow seeds of hope in the Sahara Desert.

It is a good day up to now.

People are getting excited around the table, big eyes are singing purple melodies,
and the fire fairy is still spinning the wheel.
But the casino is going to close soon and the players who had won nothing
have to turn into slaves.

The lights shut down.
The poor losers walk to the exit and the eyes of the Casino accompany
them to the lands of cruelty. Not everyone can risk so much in life,
and yet, the following morning,
hundreds of people will be waiting for their turn at the wheel of torture.

Ants Under the Moon

It was a Sunday in the late evening.
The ant family had been working all day and were about to go to bed.
The King, the Queen, and the one thousand children marched
in military step towards their house.
The forest was full of that sweet nightfall, so safe and pleasant.
The leaves of the trees swayed in the wind, whispering a happy melody
that helped the ants to stay awake.

The evening was about to fall, and the full moon would soon cover the path
with a white shadow. They had to hurry. Indeed, they had heard
that on the night of the full moon,
a crazy wolf attacked insects, especially workers.
As the night enveloped black beams on the horizon,
the ants were walking faster and faster.

The moon burst out in the middle of the woods and strident screams
of wolf divulged the danger. The ants were not far away, they ran to their refuge.
Just as they arrived at the door, the crazy wolf was there waiting for them.
He jumped on the first ant and crunched. The whole family was shaking,
holding themselves together.

The Queen engaged the wolf in a conversation to bring him to reason,
but he did not want to hear anything that would delay his feast.
When he was full, he disappeared and there were only three ants left.
The Queen and two children.

The ants had cried so much all night that in the morning, a lake had formed
at the feet of their house. They plunged into the lake and unexpectedly,
the wolf reappeared.
"Excuse me, dear ants. I regret having broken your family last night.
I was crazy, but I'm not mean."

The Queen came out of the lake, dried herself in a leaf, and called her children to work.
There was no time to lose. It was necessary to rebuild a family.
They totally ignored the wolf.

The sad wolf followed them, unhappy, miserable, helpless, not knowing
what to offer to these three poor ants so he could be forgiven.
The ants proved to be stronger, more resilient,
than the lone wolf because the ants will continue marching on together.

Brilliant Ghost

Big eyes stand out against a background of music
The ears hide the nose, the feet sing on the ceiling
The mouth wants to speak but the tongue says no!
The pale forehead folds over this mystical setting

In this terrifying dark, the right eye blinks at me
As if to reassure but I do not understand anything
The teeth stand in pairs, nothing makes sense anymore
Head disarticulated without even following lines

Strange, the nose plays the ghost
The foot plays the piano, the nails make tap dance
Bizarre thing, who are you? Alien or model?
Can you be fixed? Should we call you human?

But, oh! Drama! What am I saying? Behind my back
I feel kicks, yet the feet are up there
They shine like stars, they fly like flags
The music is growing into a drumming sound

Silence comes back, but I can not see anything
In what mysterious world have I been immersed?
Me, so simple, too simple, I am clueless
Oh! Organs, who will be my destiny?

Three Ladies Under a Radiant Sun

By a nice day of summer, in a far countryside, three ladies are talking
about their misfortune. The first one had her heart broken
by the prince of Tharaha, the second one lost a child in a boat which sunk in a storm,
and the third one is haunted by nightmares of snakes.
But the sun is shining, and they hope it will help them cope with their misery.

They did not realize they were sitting on a dog. His name is Hartanio.
He survived recently from a fight with other dogs.
He hears the despair of the women and wants to help.

Not far from the company lives Hertus, a strange animal. He is a bird with blue
feathers, a crown, and fat hands. He just moved to this part of the country in order to
find peace and serenity. He left behind both joy and sorrow. But, he brought a suitcase,
red like the radiant sun, filled with memories and remedies.

Hartanio knows this and goes to find Hertus with the hope of helping the three ladies.

Hertus takes his suitcase, opens it, and shows to Hartanio his belongings.
In the suitcase contains a pillow which is smaller than a canary head yet covers
the pictures, books, lost feathers, and some medicine. Hertus takes the pillow
and tells Hartanio to bring it under the radiant sun.
After the pillow is warmed by the sun,
each of the ladies would have to sleep on it for a short period of time.

Hartanio runs to the ladies with the pillow hung on his back and goes
to tell them of his plan. The sun is still very bright, warm, and comforting.

The three ladies sleep on the fiery pillow,
the sun turns black, and their mood is lightened.

The prince returns, the child reappears, and the nightmares vanish.

Geese of the Capitol

In ancient Rome, a long time ago, the inhabitants of a city were called
by the name Romans.
They lived peacefully in a serene atmosphere. They were rich and powerful.
But they knew there could be a danger.

Indeed, not far from there, a little city called Gaulineum
was longing for their strength.
The Gaulois started to get jealous.

So, to protect the city, at the top of a mountain,
two soldiers dressed in purple, made sure that no invaders
came to disturb their peace. Most soldiers preferred
to sleep on the open ramparts anyway.

Their dog, Saturnin, was also part of the group.
He was the guardian of the soldiers.

But one evening, around midnight, an enemy named Zarashy,
wearing an armor colored by fire, was walking towards the fort.
While he was only a few meters away, the soldiers, who had been
watching for several days with no sleep, did not wake up.
The march of the enemy did not disturb Saturnin either
who was eating his feast.
The danger was imminent.

But some geese, playing near the fort, were still awake.
They heard the noise, hollered, and began to flap their wings
which awakened the soldiers who managed to chase the impostor.
The geese saved the city and its inhabitants.

The dog has been punished to never eat human food again
and the geese got invited to a ceremony to celebrate the event.
Each year after that, on the same day, a dog is sacrificed
and a geese party rejoice in this wonderful night.

Barnyard in Disguise

It's the New Year. The snow dresses the small farm of Batancourt.
Mr. Pilm and his wife are watching the show through the window as large flakes
fly in the foliage. Flurries go gently as a carpet of white foam lands on the barn.

It is extremely cold. The animals gather around a log fire to prepare for their
evening. They were invited to a New Year's party at the neighboring farm.
There is a pig, an ant, and a goat.

The pig starts to play with the ant. He draws with his tail three magic, multicolored
butterflies while the ant marches in-step, like a soldier avoiding mines.
They both laugh and can hardly contain their joy.

"If you can be anything," said the pig to the ant, "what would you be?"

"A giant marmot," said the ant. "I have worked hard all these years and
would like to rest a bit.
"And you?" asked the ant to the pig.

"I would like to be a duck, so I can end up playing with kids in their bath.
A black duck with a long neck."

But the goat stays silent. She turns her head slowly and begins sadly to undress.
"It's time for me to tell you something. I heard the bosses talking last night,
they talked about us. They talked about selling us to the market
in exchange for firewood.
I'm sorry, the party is over."

The pig and the ant begin to sing and dance more intensely
as they circle around the goat.

"Are you insane? Do you want to die?" said the goat.

"Don't you understand that the party only begins?" answered at the same time,
the pig and the ant. "And you, my dear goat, you will be the King Duck.
You will lead us through our journey."

The three butterflies landed on each of our friends and a magic wing-stroke
transformed them into what would become their destiny.

The Crazy Octopus

In the hollow of the Atlantic Ocean, in deep sands, far from all other species,
lives an octopus tribe.

The oldest, bored by the monotony of the days, decides to go on vacation.
She brings with her an umbrella, a pipe, a guitar, a can of tomato sauce,
a pair of socks, a pen, a car tire, and an olive.
The crazy octopus has only 8 arms.
She ties her belongings to her tentacles and escapes toward other moons,
other deep waters.

On her trip, she meets a fierce shark, but she sings a song
and the shark falls asleep.
A little further, a mouse is drowning. She offers her the umbrella.
Tired, she takes shelter under a rock.
Another octopus is hiding there, and our crazy octopus is hungry.
She eats the tentacles with tomato sauce.
She falls asleep on the car tire. The next day, the water is clear as
a full moon, and the crazy octopus wakes up and continues her journey.

She meets a water rabbit who has lost his carrot.
The octopus gives him her pipe.
It starts to snow crystal bubbles. A centipede gets frozen feet.
The octopus gives him her socks.
Then she keeps going, lighter than ever, thinking that she will stop when
she has given all her effects.

She then meets an eel with glasses, thinks that it is an intellectual,
and as proof of love, she throws her ink and gives the pen to the eel.
The crazy octopus cuts the olive in half,
makes a hat with one half, a suit of armor with the other half,
and an earring with the kernel.

Her journey is over, she has nothing left to offer. Maybe her experience.
Maybe she will become a psychiatrist. The healer of the sea.

Light as a feather, she falls asleep under a shell. When she awakes,
she begins to dance, to sing, to kiss the shellfish.

Is she crazy or just in need of love?

Flowered Dog

One day, while the sky dazzled its valley of memories
with its bluish silver pearls, three dogs were heading towards
the glacial lake of Vernicourt for a picnic.

It was a winter day and the whole valley seemed lifeless.
The branches of the trees were fragile like a delicate
spirit with red shadows.

When the dogs were near the water, they sat down in a circle.
One of them proposed a game.
"Let's go look at ourselves in the water.
The one of us who will see his image reflected as clear as
the transparency of a groom's dress, will have the right with a magic paw,
to return to the past at a happy moment, which will then last forever."

The clouds began to float in the pure air and suddenly, the deluge.
Heavy rain fell on the valley of memories, a warm and melodious rain.
But the dogs could not see anymore.
The water became murky.

They went to shelter under a tree and the most fantastic of all
buried his paw in the ground, hoping that the rain would sprout
some flowers and cover his toes with exquisiteness.

He remembered the smell of lavender fields, the arrogant beauty
of sunflowers, the passion of poppies, the delicacy of acacias.
The rain did not stop.
The flowered dog fell asleep while cultivating his dream.
A storm broke. He woke up alone,
dressed in delicious scents and colors.

He went running through the valley bringing messages of love,
symbols drawn on petals that he offered to passersby
stunned by so much splendor.
Then, he disappeared in the hollow of their dreams
to go running after other spirits also eager for beauty.

The Carnival Fish

"I don't agree. I see a unicorn."
"I see a lizard," says the horse.
The duck with a long blue neck stays silent.

The carnival fish starts to go insane.
"Am I not alone here? Please, tell me. My eyes are blurred, and I can only hear
the sound of the ocean. I can only feel the cold water on my skin. All those years,
I could have communicated with you, and you stayed silent?"

Three bubbles started to dance in the water, bringing to each of them,
a message of love that has been filled by colorful loneliness.
This love that was contained for so many moons, ready to explode.
How many more bubbles will gracefully swing in the
water and touch their souls?

And the carnival fish thinks... "How lonely they must have been,
all together, with no love to share!"

Butterfly Comb

I had a dream.
All the people in the world celebrated hair day, even the bald
who were trying to hide. For that day, a prayer was made,
and the hairs floated in the air
and flew like threads of wool, balancing and dancing through the horizon.
Shampoo was drenching a fine rain on the clouds while hair bathed.

But one man on Earth kept his hair, one man who didn't pray.
He metamorphosed into a butterfly comb and went up in the sky
as a savior of the unknown world.

He was going from cloud to cloud, singing charming melodies, and pushing on
each tooth of the comb-like piano notes which were bouncing like pearls in the wind.

Each time he went through a cloud, he combed the hairs
and gave them tasks to accomplish.

A hierarchy started to form among clean hairs.
There were billions of them turning their pinheads in search of a loved one.
It was still dark, but the sun would soon rise.
Hairs were dry, and armies were marching toward the killing sun.

Suddenly, a huge yellow light covered the sky. All the hairs burned like hay in a fire.
The butterfly comb was very sad. He had done all this work for nothing.
As he fell, he screamed with fear. Faster and faster,
he finally exploded on top of a gas station.

I abruptly woke up and looked through the window.
It was snowing, and everyone was wearing hats.
It was not a dream.
I was the butterfly comb.

The Unborn Baby to the Mean Cat

You do not have a heart!
But I want to heal you.
You have no fears, but I want to give them to you,
You have no joy, but I want to offer you some.
You look like a dirty shadow that only thinks of hurting.
You do not see me. I dream of the day when I am bursting out
of my mother's heart to come to your rescue.

I learn so much from the silence of passion. When I get out,
you will be 15 years old. That is 76 years old in human age.
Like human beings, cats do not change when they get older.
Yet I know that I can heal you. My parents created me in
the wave of passion and emotion.
I will share these comforts with you.

You are mean.
Why did you devour a canary this morning?
He was chanting for you all summer.
And Miss Blaire found her socks in your bowl of milk,
just before going to an interview.

But wait. Maybe it's not too late,
maybe you can live your last years in kindness.

I'll fly out like an arrow that will pierce your
demon heart and turn you into a loving cat.
I've been watching you for months.
I have only one idea in mind when I leave my golden cage,
to redeem your purity.

Wait for me!

I know you cannot hear me. You have fun kicking me
and the more I suffer, the more I want to love you when the day comes.
You are too vain. Give back those whiskers to the neighbor's cat.
Do not make bad eyes in front of frightened babies.
They did not have my strength at birth.

One day, you will be healed, and I hope it will not be too late
to discover the joy of loving.

I am coming!

The Alcoholic Siren

Some boats navigate on the Red Sea.
The sails dance in the breeze like fragile lace under the moonlight.
It's the fish festival. They turn around the boat making circles in the water.
Salty gurgles explode like champagne bubbles and the foam forms a white blanket
over the waves. A Siren swirls in this warm and welcoming water.

The Siren has not eaten for days and drinks this saltwater like honey.
The other fish are more suspicious.
They watch her show off and stumble from pebbles of seas
into shingles of deeps.
They laugh and make fun of her. The Mermaid swims and struts, her belly full
of champagne bubbles. She is drunk.
She gives herself a show, draws odd shapes
and compliments herself on her creativity.

One of the fish calls her, "Eccentric Mermaid, where is your family?"

"I'm celebrating my divorce, it's the best day of my life,"
the alcoholic Siren answers.
"I left my lover because he thought he was the fish king when he was weak and stingy".
"He was shadowing me," she adds.
"Death is too long to be disturbed by parasites.
I am free and I am drunk. Joy is sparkling in my tummy.
I am aware of the magnitude of this event and I am happy to share it with you.
If you meet my husband, tell him that I am finally happy
and that he can forget about me.
I do not want to drink cheap wine when I know there are millions
of bubbles just waiting to light up my palate. I have luxurious tastes.
I am very attractive, I deserve better than this infamous companion
who has degraded me all my life.
So I drink.
I drink while remembering my bad days, I drink to the health of other
Mermaids imprisoned in their family. I drink to hope, to luck, to life."

It starts to rain and the sky seems to get very choleric.
The Mermaid climbs on one of the boats, goes to the dining room, staggering,
and falls asleep on a sofa under the astonished eyes of the sailors.

The day rises, the sea is calm.

Dreams Board

A crowd of people is waiting in front of a shop in the city of Rotembourd.
They have been selected by the mayor to participate in the dream lottery.
Citizens of many types wait with anticipation.

The door finally opens, revealing a large wall on which boards of dreams are depicted.

People rush in front of this amazing display.

There is not a sound. The silence draws red stars that people have to catch.
They must then kiss their star which will turn them into royalty of the night.
There, they will be in communication with the sacred spirit which will deliver
the secret to catch dreams.

The first royalty of the night, now in a large red cape, starts to swirl and flies
to touch the wall to get his dream.

He has won the dream of desire.

All future nights will envelop his spirit of wonderful wishes that he can control over
the darkness. The second prince wins the plume dream. He will write a book about
the circus of delight.
But what happens to the third prince? He cannot touch the wall.
He falls to the ground and will be haunted by nightmares of war until his death.

The red stars turn gray and the wall is covered with a black smoke
that prevents the people from observing the fantastic illustrations.
They all panic. It's dark.
There are no more stars, no more dreams, and a heavy rain falls on the city.
The Mayor of Rotembourd is charged with spirit manipulation.
He will be executed on the pyre of the city at dusk.

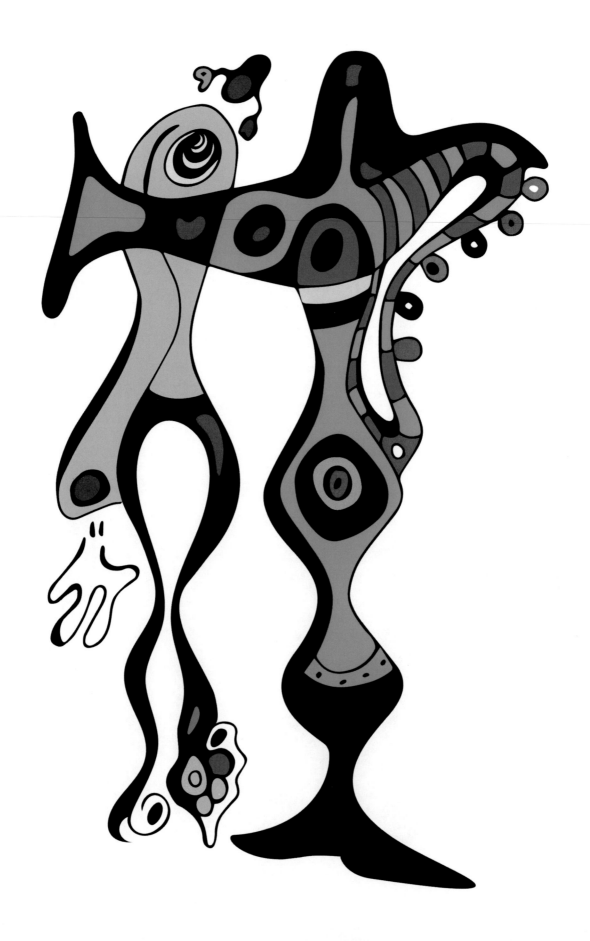

Egyptian Mermaid

Along the beach of the Mediterranean Sea, a young man wanders. Troubled by his past love story, he seeks peace, hope, and comfort. Mr. Fling has never been to a beach before.

His green coat protects him from the burning sun as he tries to forget his failure with his past lover. Tired, he sits on a rock and begins to dream of a better life.

Suddenly, a wave awakens him from his dream. Cold water on his face drives away all the bad memories. His eyes, full of sadness, open on an idyllic landscape.

A mermaid jumps out of the water and settles on the same rock as his legs.
A mermaid? Am I the victim of a hallucination?
Should I start a conversation? Will she understand? he asks of himself.

Her face reminds him of a block of carved ice with long hair that dances like a sweet melody. The mermaid begins to sing love songs. As she sings, she envelops Mr. Fling in her long blue arms, gently caressing the man's chest, and murmuring to him that he should accompany her into the deep sea.

There, they will have a perfect life. No more sorrow, only waves of joy.

Mr. Fling is tempted. After all, it's the chance of a lifetime.
Who will I miss? And who will miss me?

"Yes," he said without second thought, "let's go and visit the underwater world. I will follow you. I will love you, always. I am a good swimmer. I will cherish you, give you children, and fulfill your dreams."

"You'll never swim," the siren answered. "I'm going to transport you, it's a dangerous world out there. You will not be free. You will always need me. But, I will always be there for you.
I will not love you, I will protect you."

"I need to be loved and I need to be free!" Mr. Fling yelled to the sky.
Why do you sing love songs if you don't believe in love?"

"I sing songs of love when I am on earth and I take these beautiful words with me that make me drift from wave to wave and unimaginable depths. Fine, go get the love and freedom you desire. I will come back in ten years on this same rock. You will have one last chance. Surely then, you will be older and wiser."

The Marine Clown

It is time to swing, it is time to dance in the waves of light.
The marine clown is wearing a thin, purple coat on which
two wings are balancing his body.
A red wing and a white wing.
A wing of passion and a wing of wisdom.

A comical fish appears in front of his beak.
The fish is tempting the poor clown, who is driven by his passion for food.
The red wing is on his side, a catastrophe. This time, he doesn't want to eat the fish.
The marine clown has a lovely heart, and this fish seems quite friendly.

Can the wing of reason convince the marine clown that his real passion is
somewhere else? That dancing in the waves of light is better with a friend?

Can it drive his appetite away and let the fish live, and maybe,
the comical fish will become his companion?

The Emperor Penguin

In the depths of Antarctica, a penguin was awakened by a crying baby...
The cherub, named Zoé, was dressed in multicolored wool.
Despite his sorrow, the coat gave him an air of joy.

We, the penguins, disguised as piano notes, are always fascinated
by the glow of human beings and their colorful garments.

This penguin was not just any penguin. He was the Emperor Penguin.
His name was Pinglington. He had reached this rank after triumphing
over a balloon battle.

For each won ball, he had acquired the right to exercise a special power.
He had the power to reunite lost babies with their fathers.

The dangers of braving the way, were part of the spirituality of the pilgrimage.
He flew through the winds and the mountains, as the baby snuggled against him,
flapping little wings and humming tunes of freedom.

How lucky for this little baby to fall on the Emperor Penguin!
But there was a procedure to follow.
After finding the father, the baby should be hooked to the penguin's belly
and his father will fight a balloon battle to get his child back.
But the father could not see the baby until he won.

Pinglington found Mr. Rainbow in the middle of Time Square.
What a change from his peaceful environment! He explained the rules of the game.

Mr. Rainbow was at a disadvantage and the penguin was generally winning.
Why would Pinglington travel so far if the purpose was to keep the baby?
Well, the game was not over yet. The father had one last chance.
If he could remember how his child was dressed, he would win.

With all his heart, Mr. Rainbow was looking into his memory of how Zoé was dressed
for her last day at the nursery. He suddenly remembered.

"Mr. Pinglington, my baby was dressed in a rainbow.
A deep blue, like the marine ink, a yellow canary, a green, greener than the fresh
grass with the scent of rosemary, a violet so pure that even the geraniums would
be jealous, and a fiery red, more violent than the volcanoes at the deep end of Chile."

There was no doubt. Pinglinton, with graceful wing-shot,
launched Zoé into the arms of his father,
and took off to join his brothers and sisters in the distant horizon.

About the Author and the Art

Nathalie Gribinski

Nathalie Gribinski is a French-American artist living in Chicago, USA.
After securing a law degree in Paris, moving to Chicago in 1992,
she earned a B.A. in Art at Columbia College.
Her fine-art has evolved in lock-step with her graphic art.

A wide Egyptian eye probing you.
A giant hand waving at a flower.
A suitcase, a man, and children playing with bi-color balloons.
The Tourlicoulis world is now, trumpeting an actualized social harmony.
Curves, curves, no harsh angles. Fullest, seamless continuity.
Dreamy sensuality innocent of sexuality, a blissful world that undulates
in the Eden of childhood. Here, the snakes are innocuous
- Good and Evil not yet born or unleashed.
The Tourlicoulis alone inhabit this world.

Nathalie can be found at **www.nathaliegribinskiart.com**

If You've Enjoyed this Book, Please Check Out These Other Titles from the Catalog of Rusty Wheels Media, LLC. or visit lettersandbooks.com

Quintessential Reality

Letters Never Meant to be Read (Volume II)

Letters Never Meant to be Read (Volume I)

Contractual Obligations

Worked Stiff: Poetry and Prose for the Common

Worked Stiff: Short Stories to Tell Your Boss

Where Did You Go?: A 21st Century Guide to Finding Yourself Again

The Forge: Certified Six Sigma Green Belt Certification Program Workbook

RUSTY WHEELS MEDIA

T H E Y   K E E P   T U R N I N G

25419844R00048

Made in the USA
Lexington, KY
19 December 2018